HERGÉ
★
THE ADVENTURES OF
TINTIN
★
THE
BLACK
ISLAND

EGMONT

The TINTIN books are published in the following languages:

Alsacien	CASTERMAN
Basque	ELKAR
Bengali	ANANDA
Bernese	EMMENTALER DRUCK
Breton	AN HERE
Catalan	CASTERMAN
Chinese	CASTERMAN/CHINA CHILDREN PUBLISHING
Corsican	CASTERMAN
Danish	CARLSEN
Dutch	CASTERMAN
English	EGMONT UK LTD/LITTLE, BROWN & CO.
Esperanto	ESPERANTIX/CASTERMAN
Finnish	OTAVA
French	CASTERMAN
Gallo	RUE DES SCRIBES
Gaumais	CASTERMAN
German	CARLSEN
Greek	CASTERMAN
Hebrew	MIZRAHI
Indonesian	INDIRA
Italian	CASTERMAN
Japanese	FUKUINKAN
Korean	CASTERMAN/SOL
Latin	ELI/CASTERMAN
Luxembourgeois	IMPRIMERIE SAINT-PAUL
Norwegian	EGMONT
Picard	CASTERMAN
Polish	CASTERMAN/MOTOPOL
Portuguese	CASTERMAN
Provençal	CASTERMAN
Romanche	LIGIA ROMONTSCHA
Russian	CASTERMAN
Serbo-Croatian	DECJE NOVINE
Spanish	CASTERMAN
Swedish	CARLSEN
Thai	CASTERMAN
Tibetan	CASTERMAN
Turkish	YAPI KREDI YAYINLARI

TRANSLATED BY
LESLIE LONSDALE-COOPER AND MICHAEL TURNER

EGMONT
We bring stories to life

Artwork copyright © 1956 by Editions Casterman, Paris and Tournai.
Copyright © renewed 1984 by Casterman.
Text copyright © 1966 by Egmont UK Limited.
First published in Great Britain in 1966 by Methuen Children's Books.
This edition published in 2008 by Egmont UK Limited,
239 Kensington High Street, London W8 6SA.

Library of Congress Catalogue Card Numbers Afor 20145 and RE 205-198

ISBN 978 1 4052 0618 1

Printed in China
9 10 8

THE BLACK ISLAND

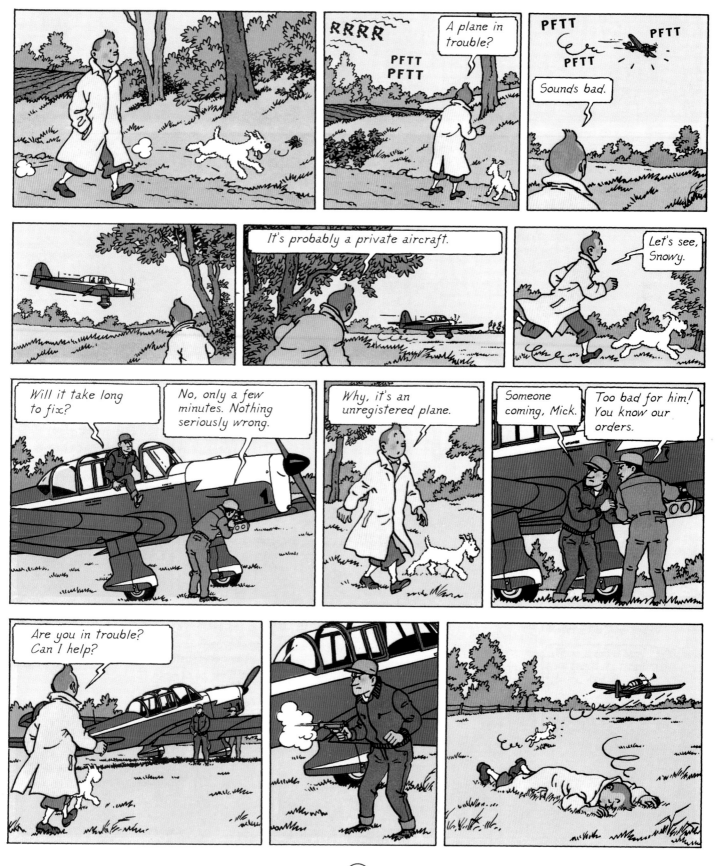

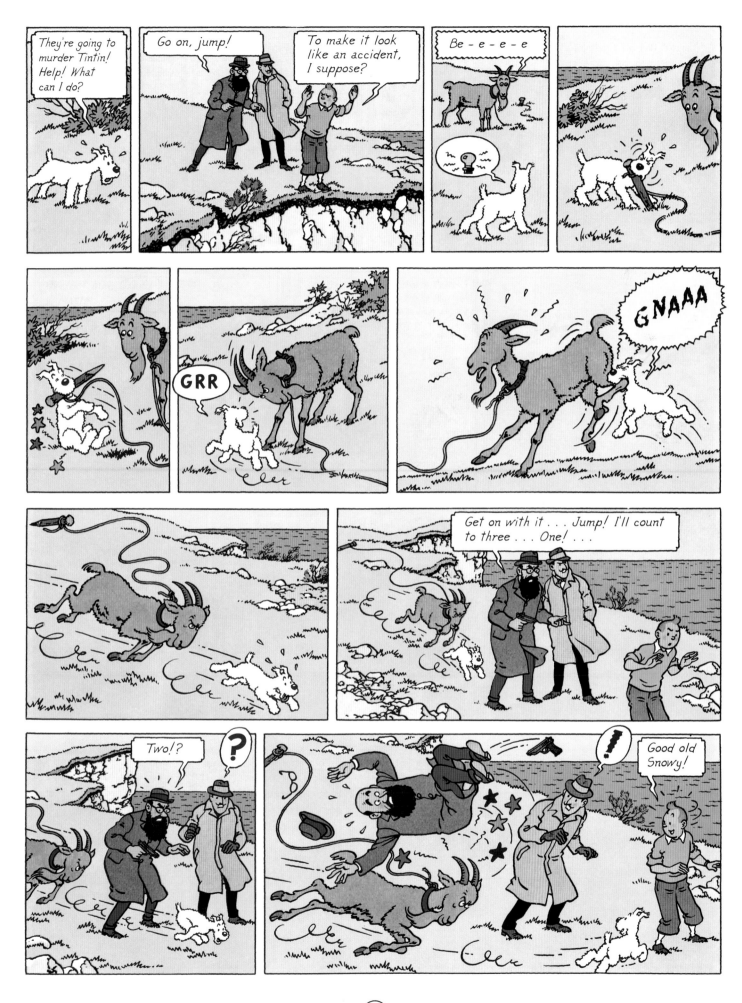

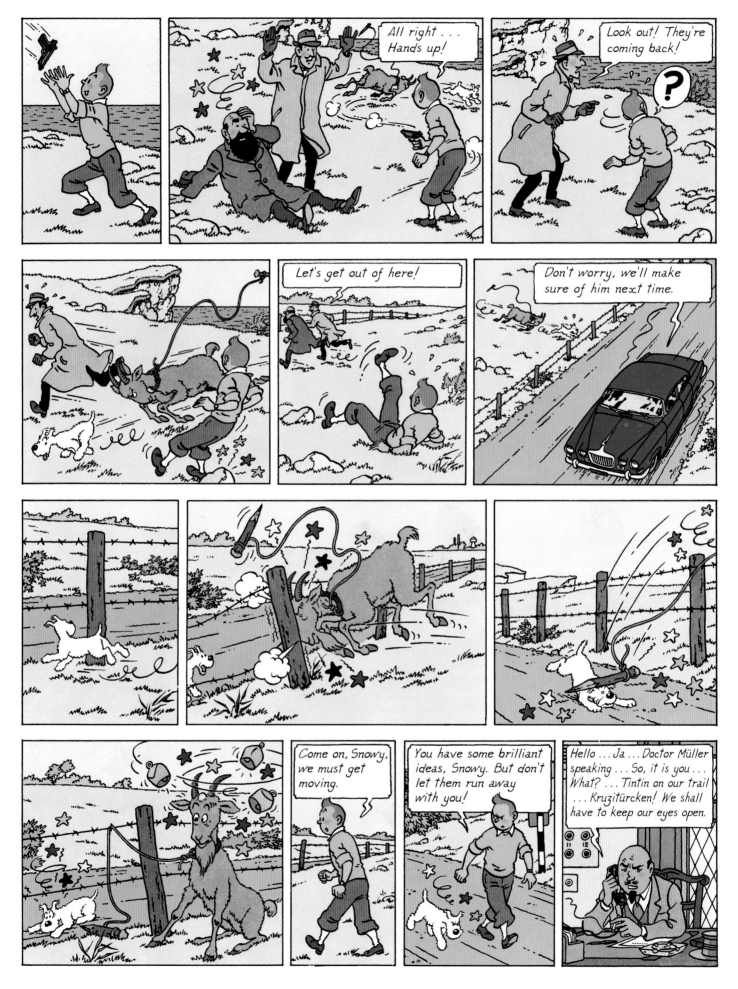

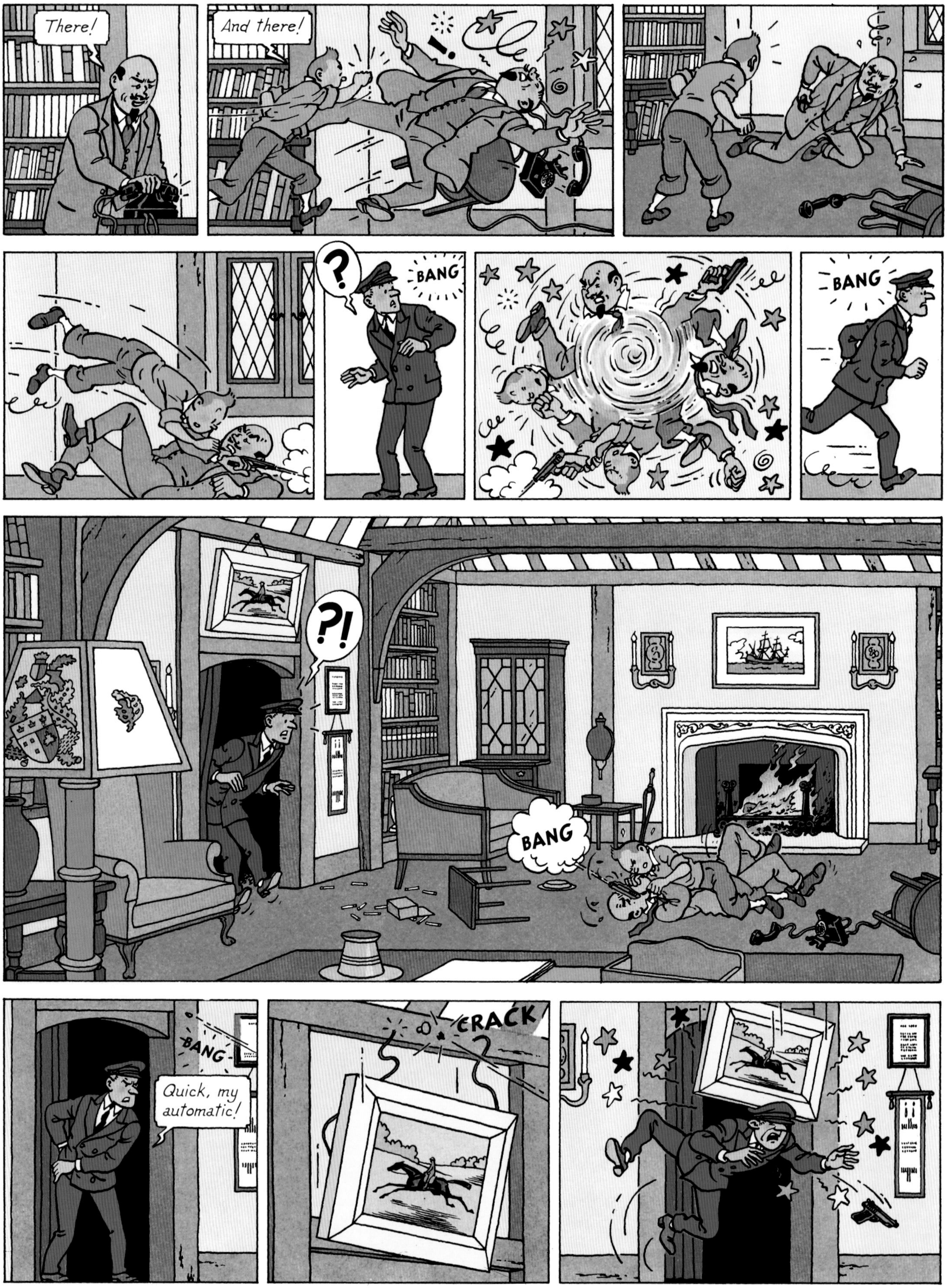
There!
And there!
BANG
BANG
?!
BANG
BANG
Quick, my automatic!
CRACK

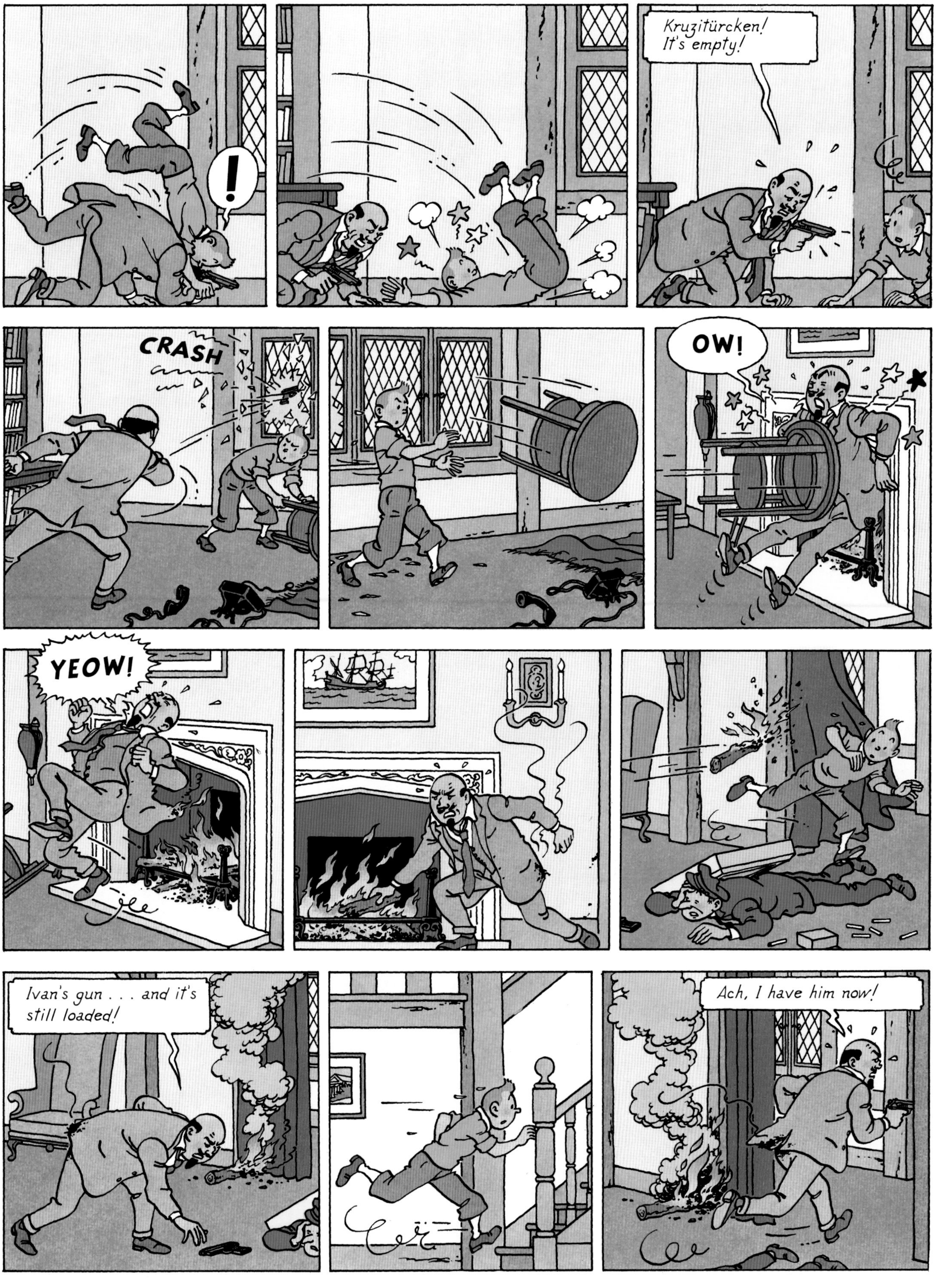
!
Kruzitürcken!
It's empty!
CRASH
OW!
YEOW!
Ivan's gun . . . and it's still loaded!
Ach, I have him now!

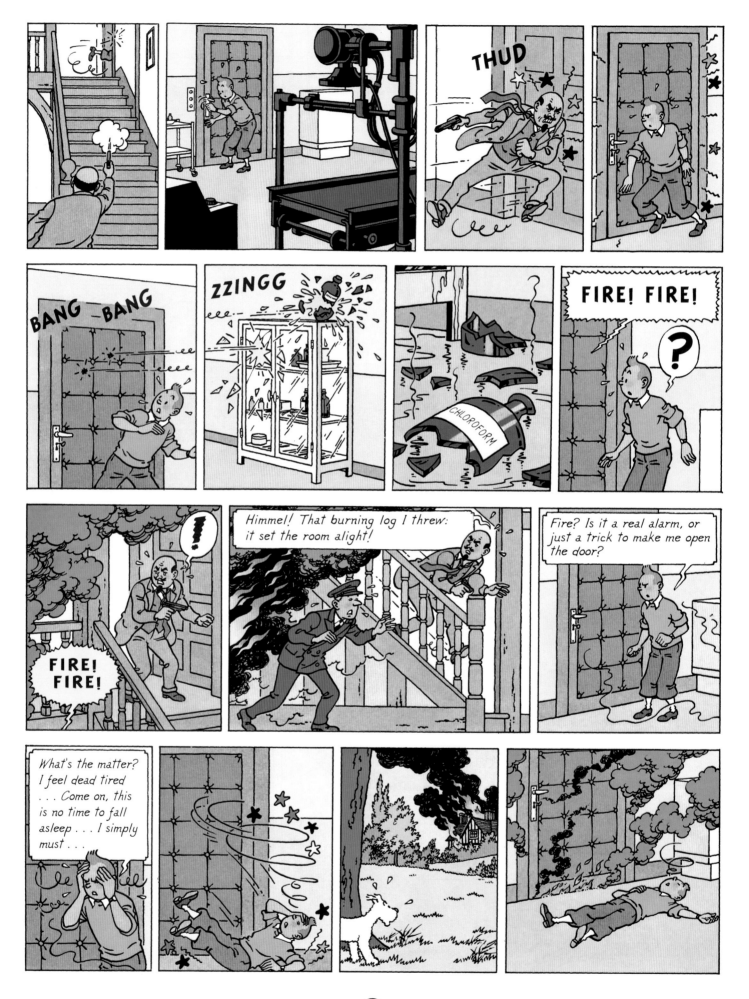

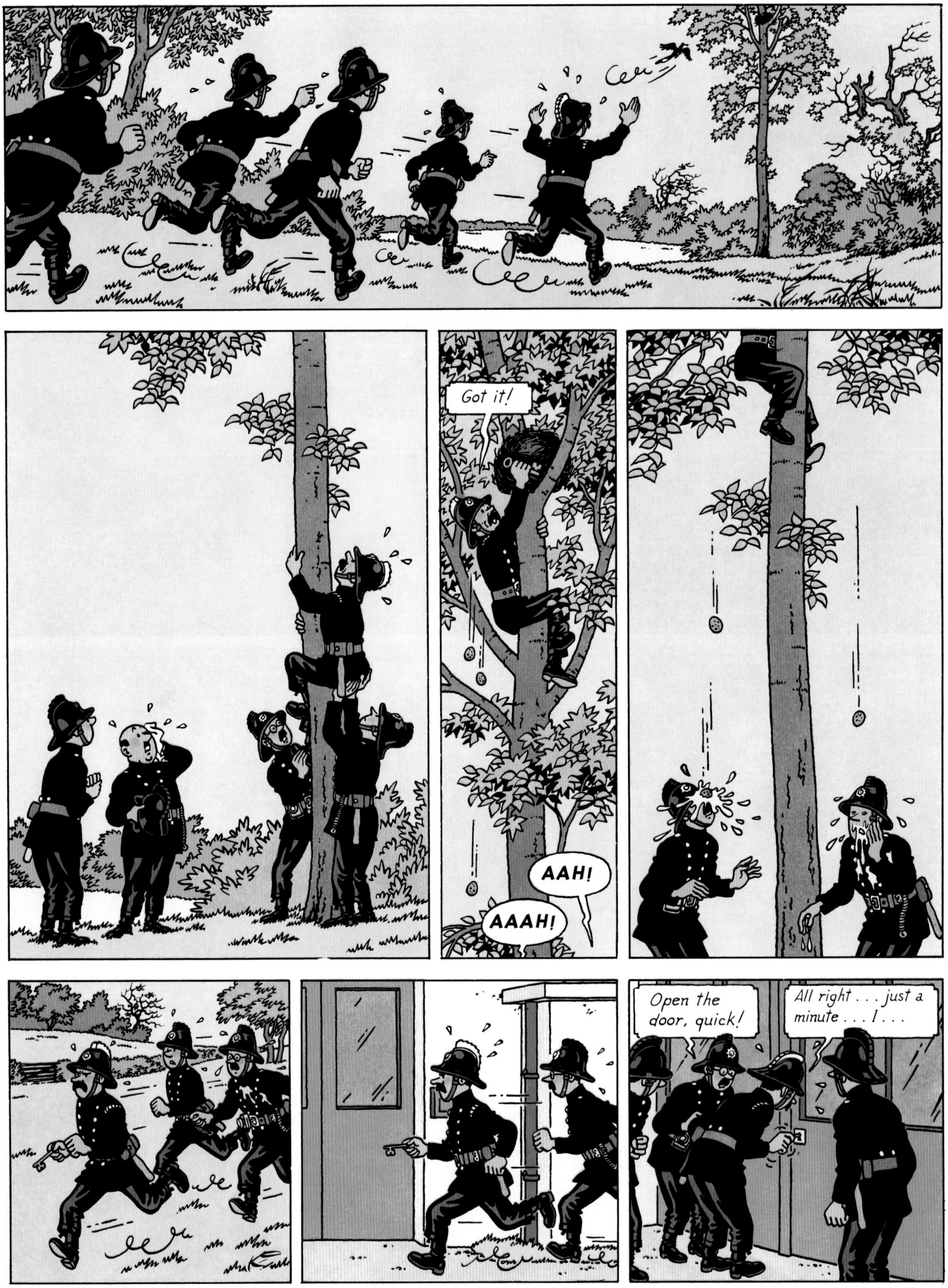
Got it!
AAH!
AAAH!
Open the door, quick!
All right . . . just a minute . . . I . . .

CRACK

?

A red beacon. I don't understand . . .

That isn't all. The wires continue along here.

I say, Tintin, are you going to do this all day?

There's another light here, too.

And now a third one . . .

The three trees are connected in a triangle . . .

GOT IT!

Müller
3 f. r.
24 - 1h.

These are instructions to the pilot in that plane. 3 f.r. △ means three flares, red, in a triangle. A signal!

Meanwhile . . .

And the worst of it is, another plane is due to deliver tonight. If the lights are not on he will go back without dropping his load. And I am running short of money . . .

We must return, Ivan. This is the plan. We enter the grounds after dark and light the beacons; the plane drops its load, which we put into the car. By tomorrow morning we can be out of the country. What do you think?

Good idea, chief.

That night . . .

Himmel! The cables have been pulled up. Someone has discovered our installation.

Look over there, chief. The beacons are alight!

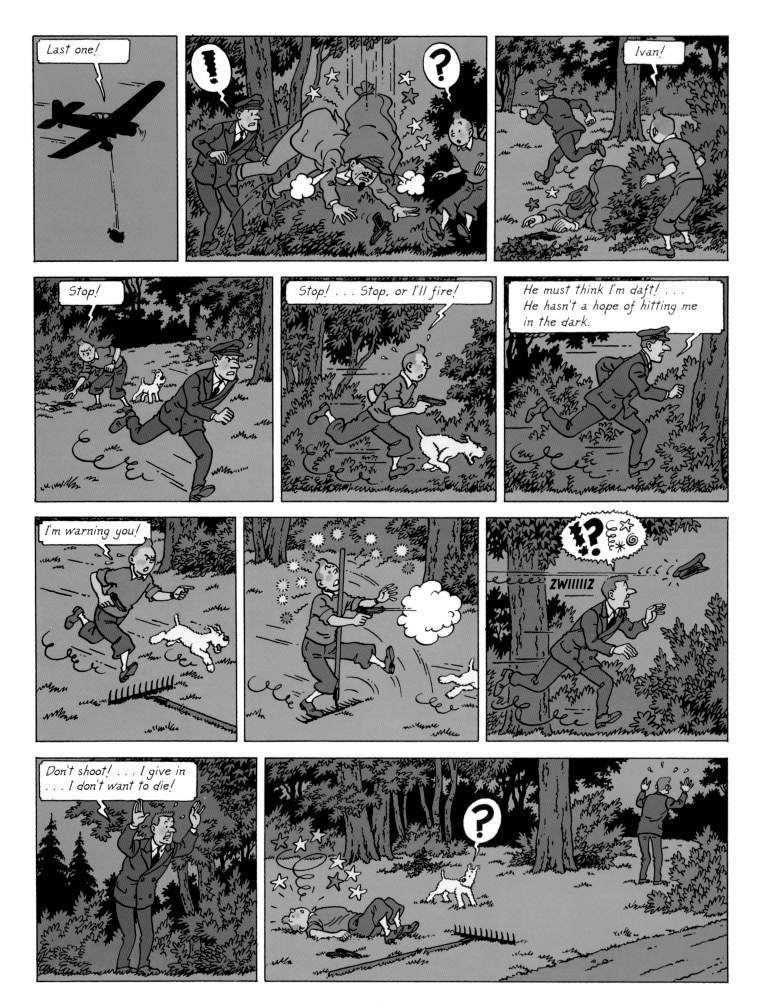

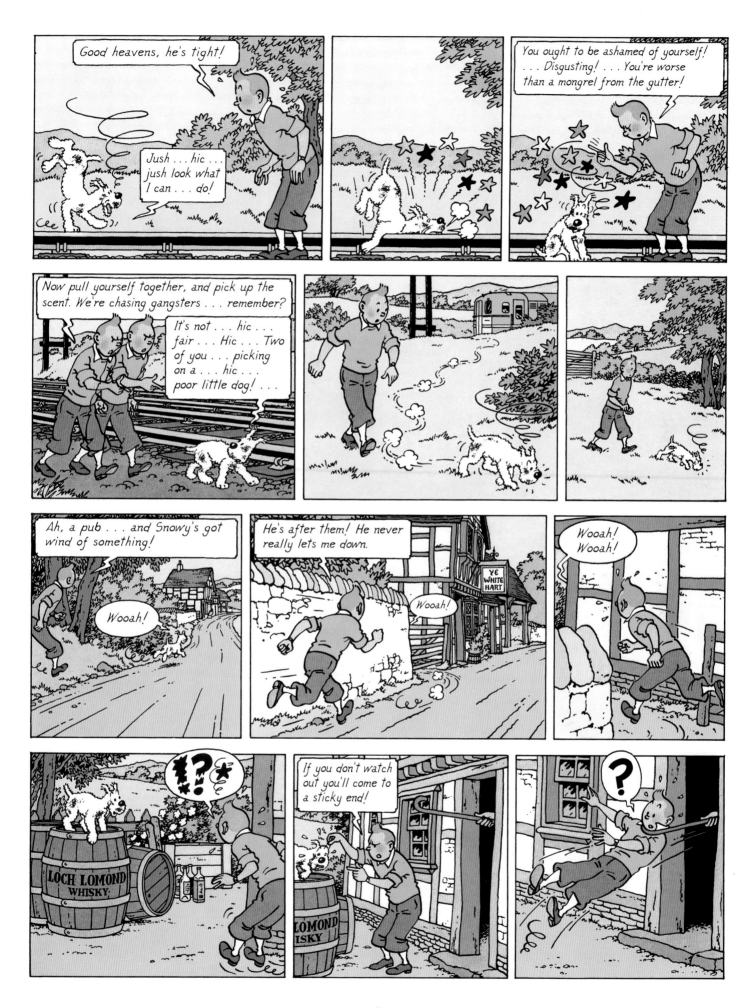

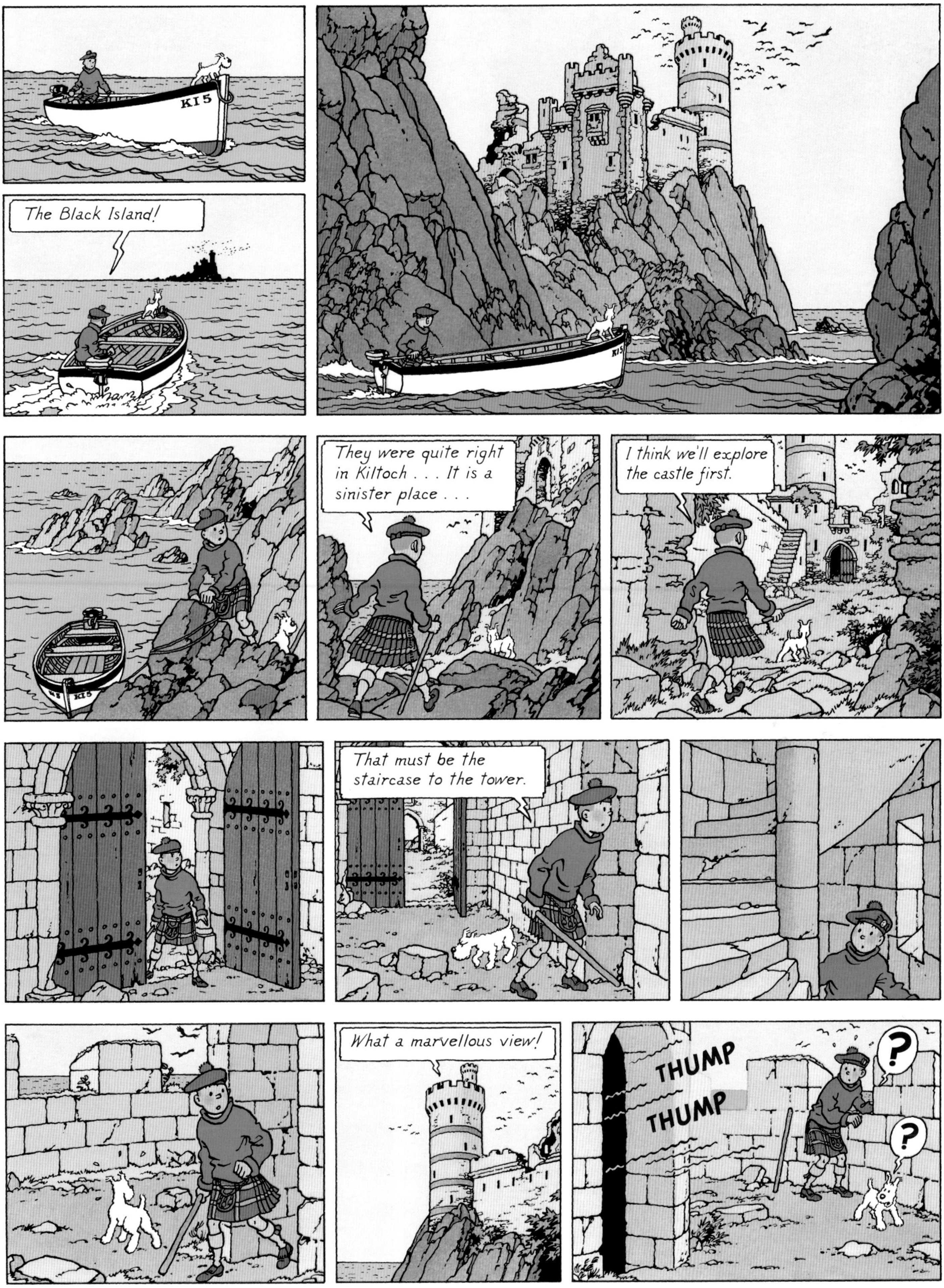
The Black Island!
They were quite right in Kiltoch . . . It is a sinister place . . .
I think we'll explore the castle first.
That must be the staircase to the tower.
What a marvellous view!
THUMP
THUMP
?
?

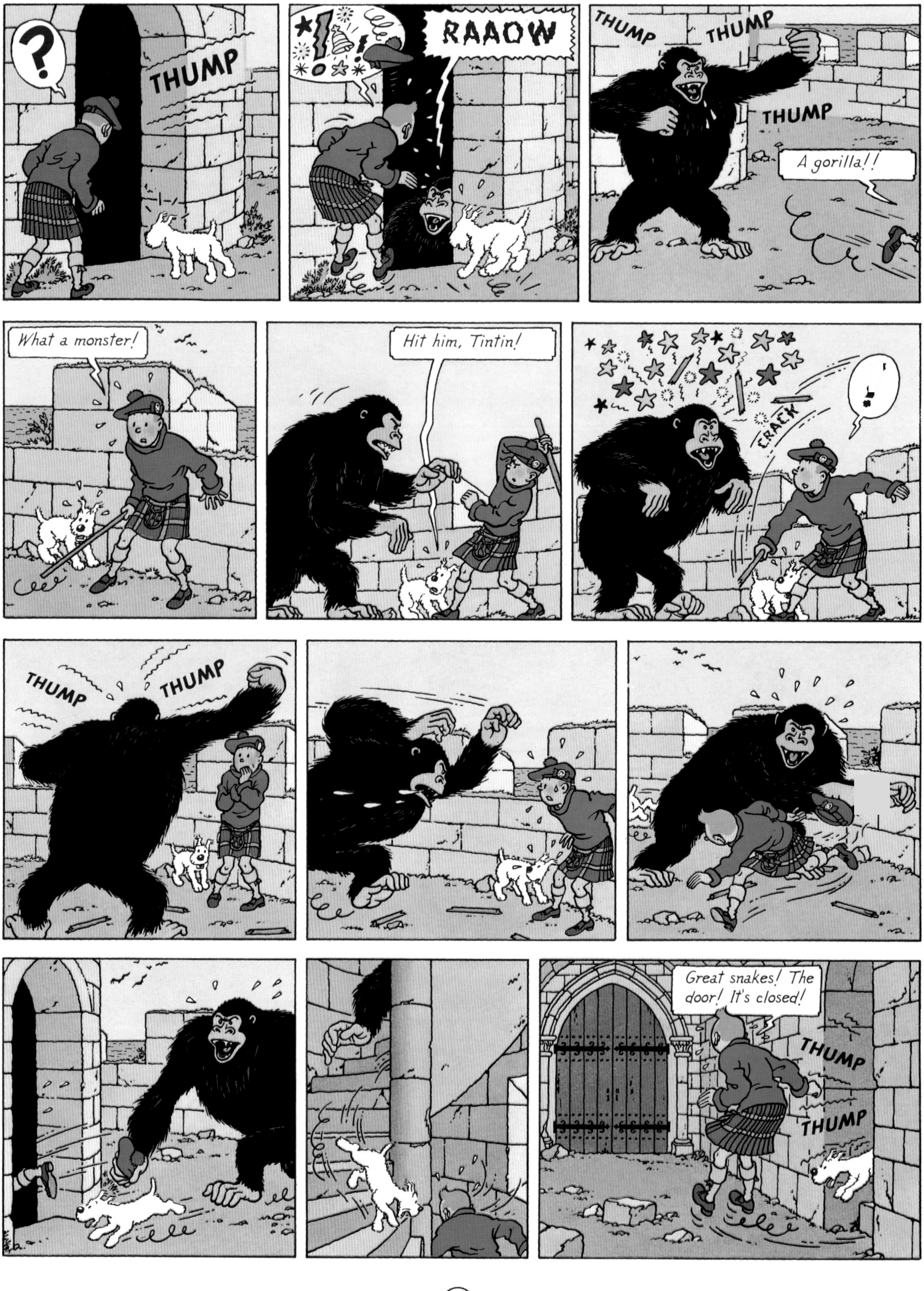
?
THUMP
RAAOW
THUMP
THUMP
THUMP
A gorilla!!
What a monster!
Hit him, Tintin!
CRACK
THUMP
THUMP
Great snakes! The door! It's closed!
THUMP
THUMP

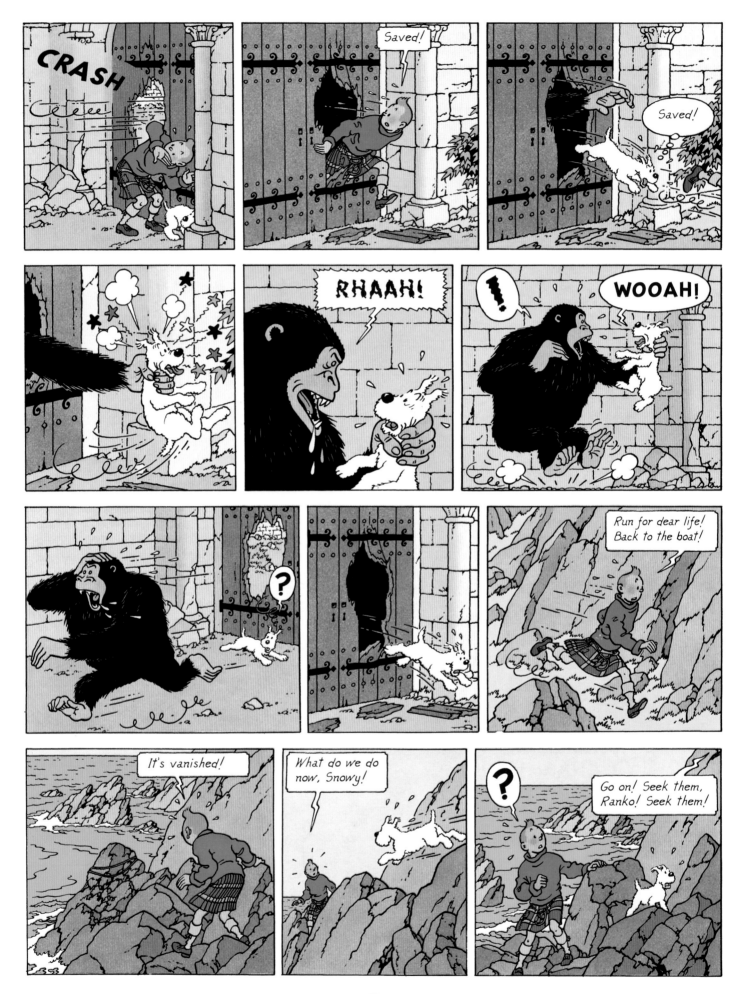

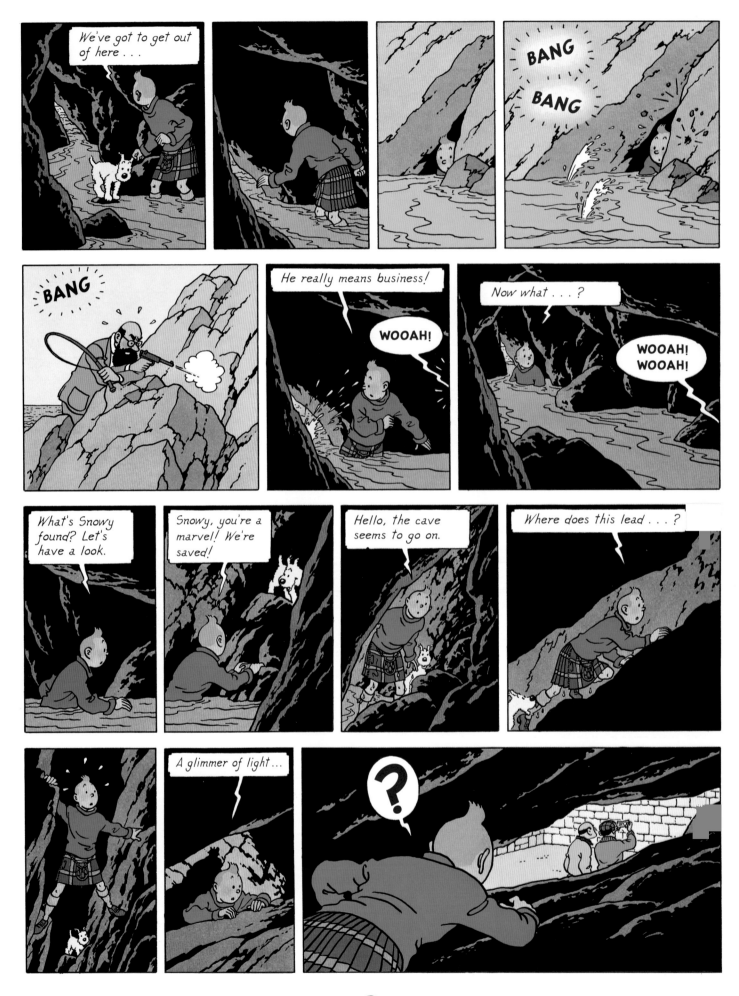

49

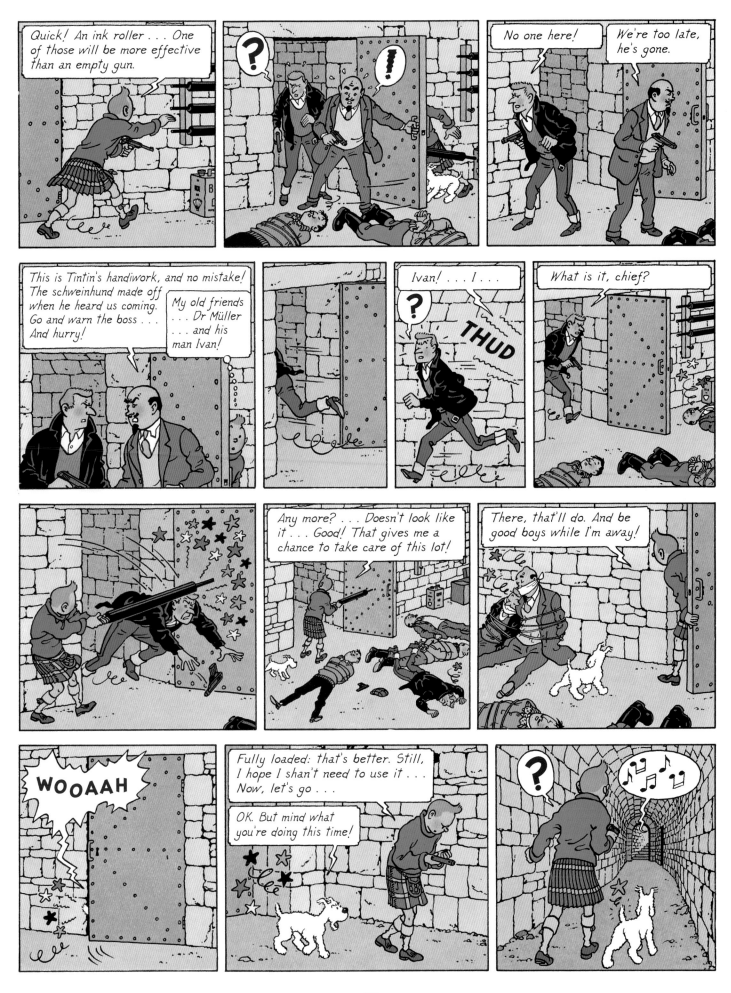

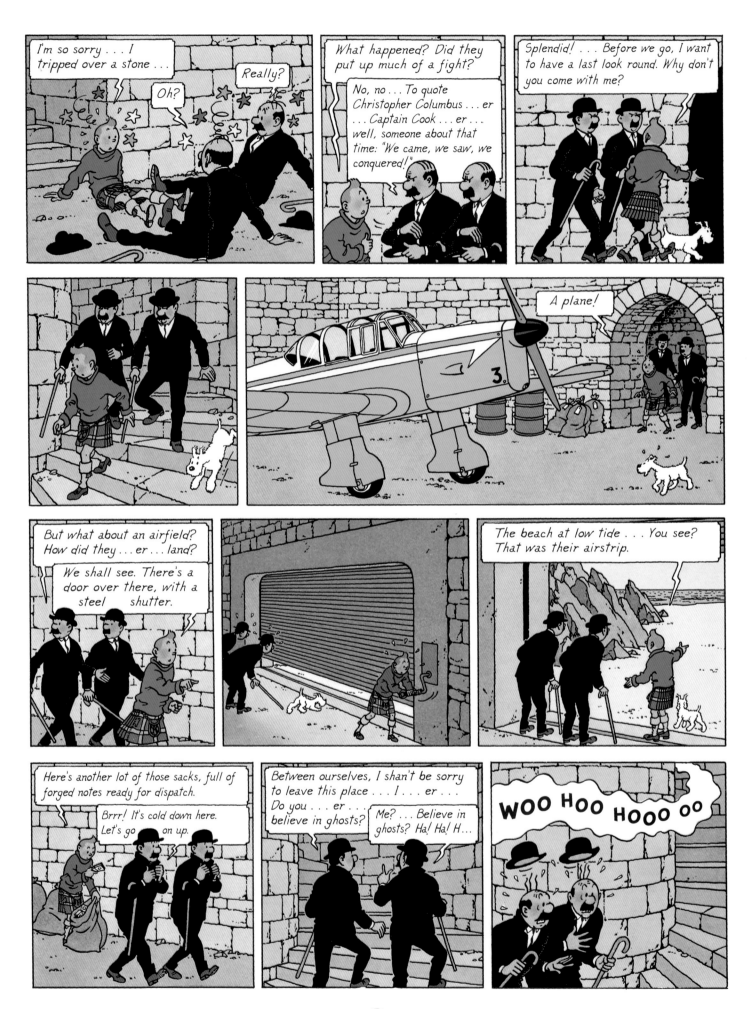

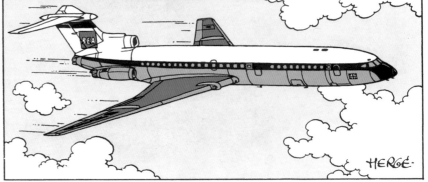